Lost Loot!

Frank, Joe, Chet, and Brian gathered around Captain Sid's chair.

Sid picked up a pipe shaped like a whale. He put it in his mouth.

The boys watched as bubbles popped out of the pipe and into the air.

"It was four hundred years ago," Captain Sid said slowly. "A pirate ship called the *One-Eyed Jack* sank off the coast of Bayport. And what was left behind was—"

"What?" Joe asked, excited. "What?"

Captain Sid leaned over in his chair and whispered. "Treasure," he said. "A chest full of buried treasure!"

The Hardy Boys® are: The Clues Brothers™

Available from MINSTREL Books

The Hardy Boys® are:

THE CLUES BROTHERS™

13

Pirates Ahoy!

Franklin W. Dixon

Illustrated by
Marcy Ramsey

A
MINSTREL®
BOOK

Published by POCKET BOOKS
New York London Toronto Sydney Tokyo Singapore

This book is a work of fiction. Names, characters, places and incidents are products of the author's imagination or are used fictitiously. Any resemblance to actual events or locales or persons living or dead is entirely coincidental.

A MINSTREL PAPERBACK *Original*

A Minstrel Book published by
POCKET BOOKS, a division of Simon & Schuster Inc.
1230 Avenue of the Americas, New York, NY 10020

ISBN: 0-671-02786-7

First Minstrel Books printing June 1999

10 9 8 7 6 5 4 3 2

THE HARDY BOYS® ARE: THE CLUES BROTHERS is a trademark of Simon & Schuster Inc.

THE HARDY BOYS, A MINSTREL BOOK and colophon are registered trademarks of Simon & Schuster Inc.

Cover art by Thompson Studio

Printed in the U.S.A.

QBP/✕

1

Smooth Sailing—Not!

Check out all the boats," nine-year-old Frank Hardy said as he ran toward the Bayport Marina.

His eight-year-old brother, Joe, looked at the docks. They were filled with power-boats and sailboats.

"They're awesome, all right," he said.

"Hey, you guys. I think I see a beached whale," their friend Chet Morton said. He pointed to a spray of water. "Thar she blows! Thar she blows!"

"Chet," Frank said. "Someone is watering the grass."

Chet stopped jumping up and down. "Oh . . . yeah," he said.

It was the first Monday during summer vacation. The Hardys' friend Brian Ludlow had invited them on his dad's sailboat. Mr. Ludlow owned the Bayport Marina and several boats.

"Are you sure this is a good idea?" Joe asked as they waited for Brian.

"Why?" Frank asked. "You're not scared, are you?"

"Nah," Joe said. He turned his baseball cap backward. "But what if the most fantastic mystery comes up while we're away at sea?"

Frank smiled. He and his brother loved solving mysteries. Their friends liked to call them the Clues Brothers.

"Joe's right," Chet said. He considered himself a detective-in-training. "What if a spy plane crashes in Bayport? While we're halfway around the world?"

"You guys!" Frank cried. "We're only going for three hours."

"Ahoy, mates," a voice called out.

The boys turned and saw Brian Ludlow. He was dressed in a white polo shirt and beige shorts.

"Hi, Brian," Frank said. "Which boats belong to your dad?"

Brian began to point. "The powerboat, the Jet Ski, and the kayaks. But we're going on that sailboat over there."

Frank and Joe stared at the shiny blue sailboat. Mr. Ludlow was already on board, raising the tall white sail.

"Not too shabby," Frank said with a smile.

Joe smiled, too. "I guess a break from detective work isn't such a bad idea."

Frank, Joe, and Chet followed Brian to the boat. There was a pile of bright orange life vests on the dock.

"Hi, boys," Mr. Ludlow said. "Ready for a sail?"

Chet snapped his feet together and gave a salute. "Aye, aye, Captain!"

First Mr. Ludlow showed the boys how to fasten their life vests. Then they each stepped into the sailboat.

"The front of the boat is called the bow," Mr. Ludlow explained. "The back is called the stern. You're standing on the deck."

"The bow, the stern, the deck," Joe repeated. "Got it."

"Any questions?" Mr. Ludlow asked.

"Yeah," Chet said. "Where are we sailing today? Hawaii? China? Africa?"

Mr. Ludlow laughed. "How about just around the bay?"

Chet shrugged. "It's a start."

The boys waited while Mr. Ludlow untied the boat. It began to rock gently.

"Maybe we'll see all kinds of neat fish out on the bay!" Joe said excitedly.

The boat began to rock some more.

"Fish?" Chet gulped. He covered his mouth with his hand. Then he burped.

"Chet?" Frank asked. "Are you okay?"

Chet burped again, this time much louder.

"Ugh," Brian said. "Stop being so gross, Morton."

"Wait a minute," Joe said. He pointed to Chet's face. "He's turning green. Like spinach."

"Spinach?" Chet groaned. He leaned forward and groaned. "I think I'm going to . . . barf."

"Dad!" Brian shouted.

"What's wrong?" Mr. Ludlow asked. He hurried over.

"It's Chet, Mr. Ludlow," Frank said. "I think he's a little seasick."

"Seasick?" Mr. Ludlow asked. He scratched his head. "But we haven't even left the dock."

"And we probably never will," Brian groaned.

"I'll be okay," Chet promised. "Maybe I'm just a little hungry."

"When *aren't* you hungry?" Joe joked. Chet was always snacking on something.

"It *is* close to lunchtime," Mr. Ludlow admitted. "Why don't you boys go up to

5

Marina Lane and grab something good to eat? Like sandwiches."

Chet grinned. "With onion rings on the side? And milk shakes?"

"I think Chet's feeling better now," Joe whispered to Frank.

Mr. Ludlow gave the boys permission to walk to Marina Lane. It was a small street filled with shops and snack stands.

The boys were going to buy sandwiches, but they changed their minds. Instead they bought burgers at the Salty Dog Snack Shack. They carefully carried them to a table under a tree.

"I should have asked for some cole slaw," Chet said as he squirted gobs of ketchup on his cheeseburger.

"For someone who was about to hurl, you sure got over it," Frank said.

"There's nothing a good cheeseburger can't cure," Chet said. He bit into his burger and chewed hungrily.

"Look," Joe said. He pointed to a boy in a yellow T-shirt. "There's Kevin Saris."

Eight-year-old Kevin was another friend of the Hardys and Chet. His parents owned Pizza Paradise on Bay Street. He was also a reporter for the Bayport Elementary School newspaper.

"Hey, Kevin!" Frank called.

"Hi, guys," Kevin said. He walked over.

"How come you're not at the pizza parlor?" Frank asked. "Don't you usually help your parents in the summer?"

"Yeah," Joe said. "Tying garlic knots, filling cheese shakers, smacking dough—"

"Not this summer," Kevin interrupted. "I have much more important things to do."

"What could be more important than pepperoni pizzas?" Chet asked.

"This," Kevin said. He pointed to an emblem on his T-shirt. "I've joined the *Pee Wee Press.*"

"You mean that newspaper that's written by kids?" Brian asked.

Kevin nodded. "I'm going to be an investigative reporter for the whole summer."

"An investigative reporter?" Joe asked. "Sounds like detective work."

"What are you investigating?" Frank asked Kevin.

"Shhhh," Kevin whispered. He looked over both shoulders. Then he sat down and leaned over. "I'm investigating the Salty Dog Snack Shack."

"You mean where we just bought our burgers?" Chet asked.

"Oh, great," Brian groaned. "Don't tell me they found chopped-up spiders in the burger meat!"

"Worse," Kevin said. "I got a hot tip that they're pouring cheap ketchup into the expensive Krantz ketchup bottles."

Joe lifted the top part of his bun. He sniffed the ketchup.

"You mean this isn't Krantz?" he asked. "It *smells* like Krantz."

"That's all part of the trick," Kevin said with a grin. "The brand they use doesn't even have a name."

"No way!" Joe said.

8

"That stinks!" Chet said. "I should have asked for mustard."

Kevin stood up. He pulled a pad and pencil from his pocket.

"When this story breaks," he said, "ketchup will never be the same again."

"Good luck," Frank called as Kevin walked back to the Salty Dog.

"Wow," Brian said. "They should call it the *Sneaky* Dog."

"That's for sure," Chet said.

Joe was about to take a bite of an onion ring when he heard a strange noise.

"SQUAAAAAWK!"

The boys looked at each other. Then the squawky voice began to sing:

"Krantz, Krantz. Really neat. Pour it on the food you eat! Squaaaaawk!"

"It's the Krantz ketchup theme song," Chet said. "But who—"

"Check it out!" Frank shouted. He pointed to a colorful bird flying their way. It flapped its big wings and landed right on Joe's baseball cap.

"Awesome," Kevin said.

"Smooth landing," Chet said.

"You guys?" Joe asked slowly. He looked up and gulped. "What . . . is it?"

"It's a parrot," Frank said. "But where did it come from?"

2

Mystery for Sale

I don't know where he came from," Joe said. He felt the parrot hop from his head to his arm. "But now I have to clean my new baseball cap."

Joe shook his head and put the cap in his pocket.

"Polly want a cracker?" Chet asked the parrot. "Or an onion ring? How about an ice cream sandwich?"

The parrot looked at Chet and blinked.

"Hey, wait a minute," Brian said. "I know that bird."

"Who is he?" Frank asked.

"It's Horatio Crackerblower," Brian said. "And he belongs to Captain Sid."

"Captain Sid! Captain Sid!" the parrot squawked. "Arrrrk!"

"He's the owner of Captain Sid's Treasure Cove," Brian explained. "It's a shop that sells sailing souvenirs."

"I didn't know Bayport had a sailing souvenir shop," Joe said. "Let's check it out."

"Don't bother," Brian said. "All Sid sells is tacky old junk."

"Tacky?" Chet said. He gave a thumbs-up sign. "That's the best kind."

Frank stroked Horatio's feathers. "Whether we buy anything or not, we have to return Horatio," he said.

"Home!" Horatio squawked. "Ohhh, boy!"

Brian led the way to Captain Sid's Treasure Cove. It was a small store at the end of Marina Lane.

The paint on the door was chipped. The

display window was so dusty that Frank and Joe could hardly see into it.

A small bell above the door rang as they walked inside.

"It's dark in here," Chet whispered.

"And it smells like a musty attic," Joe said. He felt a sneeze coming on. "Ahhh-chooo!"

The sneeze made Horatio fly from Joe's arm onto a tall wooden perch.

"Captain Sid?" Frank called.

"Anybody home?" Joe called.

When nobody answered, the boys looked around the shop.

"This stuff is neat," Joe said.

There were shelves filled with plastic fish, seashells, and ships inside bottles.

"You like this kind of stuff?" Frank asked.

Joe's eyes lit up when he saw a model of a sailing ship.

"I like *that!*" he said.

The boys surrounded the table where the model sat. The ship was made of wood and had six sails. Two small bottles fit into holes on the deck.

"It's a salt and pepper holder," Brian said. "Tacky, tacky, tacky."

"It's also a model of an old pirate ship," Frank said. "It has a skull and crossbones on the flag."

"That's what they called a Jolly Roger," Joe said.

"The skeleton's name is Roger?" Chet asked Joe. "How do you know?"

"I saw a TV show about pirates last week," Joe said. "It was awesome."

"Awesome! Awesome! Squaaawwwk!" Horatio squawked.

Just then a voice called out from the back. "Horatio? Is that you, my friend?"

The boys watched as a man stepped from behind a fishnet curtain. His hair was gray. He wore a striped shirt and a white sailor's hat.

"That must be Captain Sid," Frank whispered.

"Are you sure?" Joe asked. "He looks more like Popeye."

15

"Ahoy, landlubbers!" the man greeted them. "Welcome to Captain Sid's Treasure Cove. I'm Captain Sid."

"Hi," Frank said. "We were just looking at your . . . merchandise."

Horatio flapped his wings and screeched. "Tacky junk! Tacky junk! Tacky junk! Tacky—"

"Shut your beak!" Chet hissed.

Captain Sid began to laugh. "I see you've met my first mate, Horatio."

Joe nodded. "He sure likes to talk."

"How come he knows the Krantz ketchup theme song?" Chet asked Sid.

"Horatio always repeats what he hears," Captain Sid explained. "And he hears lots of commercial jingles on my TV set."

Joe walked up to Captain Sid. "Are you a real sea captain?" he asked.

Captain Sid sat down on a tattered chair and leaned back.

"I've sailed all over the world," he exclaimed. "Around the coast of Florida! All the way to India! To the far continent of Africa!"

Chet wrinkled his nose. "And you landed up in Bayport?"

"Aye," Captain Sid said. "Every port is an adventure for an old salt like me."

Joe smiled. He thought Captain Sid was cool. Corny but cool.

"Speaking of sailing," Frank said, "we have to go now."

"You will come back," Captain Sid asked. "Won't you?"

The boys looked at each other.

"Um . . . " Brian said.

"Er . . . " Chet said.

"We'll be kind of busy all summer," Frank said quickly.

"Yeah," Joe said. "My brother, Frank, and I are detectives. We'll probably be solving all kinds of mysteries."

"They're the Clues Brothers," Chet said proudly.

"Brothers?" Captain Sid asked. He looked at Frank and Joe. "You two don't look like brothers."

The Hardys were used to hearing that.

Frank had dark brown hair and dark brown eyes. Joe had blond hair and blue eyes.

"Let's get out of here," Brian whispered. "My dad's waiting."

The boys began walking toward the door when Captain Sid jumped up.

"Wait," he called. "You like mysteries? I have a mystery for you that'll curl your barnacles."

The boys stopped and turned around.

"A mystery?" Joe asked. "What mystery?"

"I'd be happy to tell you," Captain Sid said with a grin. "But mysteries are for customers only."

"I think he wants us to buy something," Brian told his friends.

"No problem," Joe said. He pointed to the model of the pirate ship. "How much?"

"Fifteen dollars," Captain Sid said. He winked. "For another fifty cents, I'll fill the shakers with salt and pepper."

Joe checked his pockets. "I only have three dollars."

"That'll get you the salt and pepper," Captain Sid said. "But not the ship."

Chet walked over to one of the shelves. He picked up a green rubber whale. "Does this do anything?" he asked.

"Aye," Captain Sid said. "Moby Squirt spurts ketchup from his blowhole."

"What a brilliant idea," Chet said.

Brian reached into his pocket and pulled out a five-dollar bill. He gave it to Captain Sid.

"That's for Chet's whale," he said. "Now tell us the mystery. Please."

"Okay, okay," Captain Sid said. He sat down again. "Don't shiver yer timbers."

Frank, Joe, Chet, and Brian gathered around Captain Sid's chair.

Sid picked up a pipe shaped like a whale. He put it in his mouth.

The boys watched as bubbles popped out of the pipe and into the air.

"It was four hundred years ago," Captain Sid said slowly. "A pirate ship called the *One-Eyed Jack* sank off the coast of Bayport. And what was left behind was—"

"What?" Joe asked, excited. "What?"

Captain Sid leaned over in his chair and whispered. "Treasure," he said. "A chest full of buried treasure!"

3

Whale of a Tale

Buried treasure?" Frank asked. "Here? In Bayport?"

"Who buried it?" Joe asked.

"The notorious high-sea robber Captain Crook," Sid explained. He pointed to a portrait hanging above his chair. "There he is. Meaner than a shark with a toothache."

Frank and Joe looked at the portrait. Captain Crook was painted with bright colors on black velvet. His eyes were as round as two Frisbees.

"You think that's really him?" Frank whispered.

"Nah," Brian whispered back. "I painted the same picture in a color-by-number set."

"Well, I think it's real," Joe insisted. He turned to Sid. "Tell us more, Captain Sid."

"Yeah," Chet said. "Like why did they bury the loot in the first place?"

"To keep it safe," Captain Sid explained. "Pirates would hide their treasure, draw a map, and return for it later. When the coast was clear."

"There must be a map for Captain Crook's treasure," Joe said.

Captain Sid puffed his bubble pipe. "The map has never been found. And neither has the treasure."

"I've lived in Bayport all my life," Brian said. "I never heard about any buried treasure."

"So how do *you* know about it, Captain Sid?" Frank asked.

Captain Sid smiled. "The sea has many secrets," he said.

The shop became very quiet. All Frank and Joe could hear were bubbles popping.

"Pirates in Bayport?" Frank finally said. "Why would they come here?"

"It's possible," Joe insisted. "The TV show said that pirates sailed all over the world."

"You guys," Brian complained. "We have to go back to my dad. We're supposed to go sailing today, remember?"

"Oh, yeah," Joe said, disappointed. He wanted to stick around to hear more about the buried treasure.

"Wait up," Chet said. He ran over to the shelf. "I have to get Moby Squirt."

Chet grabbed the whale.

SQUOOSH!

"Look out!" Chet shouted.

The boys covered their eyes. Spurts of ketchup shot out of the whale and all over the shop.

"ARRRK! ARRRK!" Horatio screeched as

a glob of ketchup hit him on the wing. Another clump landed on his beak.

"Horatio!" Captain Sid said. "Are you all right?"

Chet dropped the whale. More ketchup squirted out as it hit the floor.

"Yuck!" Joe said.

Ketchup dripped from the ceiling, walls, and even the portrait of Captain Crook!

"We'd better get out of here," Frank said. "Fast."

"Good idea," Joe said.

The boys raced out of the store. Chet licked his ketchup-covered fingers as they ran down Marina Lane.

"At least it's Krantz," he said.

When they reached the marina they collapsed on the sand.

"Pirates in Bayport." Brian laughed. "Did you ever hear anything so goofy?"

"Why would they come here?" Chet chuckled. "To go to Pizza Paradise?"

"Cut it out, you guys," Joe said. "I think the story's true."

Just then Frank saw something sticking out of the sand. It was round and silver.

"I just found a quarter," Frank said. He picked it up. "Am I lucky or what?"

Joe stared at the silver coin in his brother's hand. "That's no quarter, Frank."

"Then what is it?" Frank asked.

Joe leaned over to get a closer look. His eyes opened wide.

"It looks just like a silver coin I saw on the TV show," he said. "A piece of eight."

The boys stood up.

"A piece of what?" Chet asked.

"Pieces of eight were old Spanish coins that pirates stole from ships," Joe explained.

Frank rolled the coin in his palm. "It does look really old," he said.

"And the edges are bent," Chet added.

"Look," Brian said. He pointed to the face of the coin. "There's an old sailing ship on it. And a crown."

The boys passed the coin back and forth. When it was in Joe's hand, he gave the coin a flip.

"Now do you believe Captain Sid?" he asked with a grin.

"I do now," Frank said.

"Buried treasure in Bayport!" Chet cried. He pumped his fist in the air. "Woo! Woo! Woo!"

4

Hurried Treasure

The coin is the first clue," Frank said excitedly. "The whole treasure chest can't be far away."

"And the Clues Brothers are going to find it," Joe said. "Ye-es!"

Just then a bell clanged. It was Brian's father calling them back to the boat.

"Time to shove off, crew," Mr. Ludlow called.

"You mean get back on the boat?" Chet gulped. "And get seasick again?"

Brian planted his hands on his hips. "Are you guys coming or not?" he asked.

Frank and Joe looked at each other. They knew they were both thinking the same thing. How could they go sailing when they had one of the coolest mysteries to solve?

"Sorry, Brian," Frank said. "We have to start looking for that treasure."

"Yeah," Joe said. "Things like this only come up every four hundred years."

"Okay, okay," Brian said. "But you have to promise me something."

"What?" Chet asked.

Brian grinned. "When you find the loot, save some for me."

"You got it," Frank said.

Frank, Joe, and Chet watched as Brian returned to the boat.

"Okay," Joe said. He rubbed his hands together. "Where do we start?"

"Let's do some research at the library," Frank suggested. "Maybe we can find something about the buried treasure."

"Research during summer vacation?"

Chet groaned. He grabbed his stomach. "I think I feel sick again."

The boys called home and got permission from their parents to walk to the Bayport Library.

They were just climbing the steps when a girl came running down. She was balancing a pile of books with both arms. The pile was so high that it covered her whole face.

"That's my sister, Iola," Chet said. "I'd know those yellow sneakers anywhere."

"Iola," Joe shouted. "Look out!"

It was too late.

"Ooof!"

Iola crashed right into Frank. Her pile of books fell from her arms and scattered all over the steps.

"Why don't you watch where you're going?" Chet shouted.

"With twenty books in my hands?" Iola shouted back. "You try!"

"Did you leave any books for us?" Joe teased.

"Very funny," Iola said. "I have to read all these books if I'm going to win the library's reading contest."

"Reading contest?" Frank repeated.

"The kid who reads the most books this summer wins a brand-new CD-ROM encyclopedia," Iola explained.

"Neat!" Chet said. "If you win, can I use it, too?"

"I guess so." Iola sighed.

"Then what are you waiting for?" Chet asked. He scooped up some books. "Start reading."

The boys helped Iola pick up the books. But Frank froze when he reached for a book with a blue cover.

"What is it?" Joe asked.

"This book is called *The Pirates of Bayport*," Frank said.

"*Pirates of Bayport?*" Joe asked. He smiled. "Bingo!"

"Read it out loud, Frank," Chet said. "Excuse me!" Iola said. She snatched the book from Frank's hand. "I have to start reading *right now*."

"Why that book?" Frank asked.

"It's the first one on my list," Iola said.

Chet waved his arms in the air. "Give me a break!"

Iola picked up her pile of books. "You *do* want me to win the encyclopedia, don't you?" she asked.

The boys watched Iola walk down the library steps.

"You do want me to win, don't you?" Chet mimicked. "Sisters."

"It's cool, Chet," Frank said. "We have all the information we need."

"Yeah," Joe agreed. "That book proves that there *were* pirates in Bayport."

"Ye-es!" Chet said. "Buried treasure here we come!"

"Pirates?" asked a voice. "Treasure?"

The boys whirled around. Kevin Saris stood on the steps. He was holding a book called *Cooking with Ketchup.*

"Did you just say there were pirates here in Bayport?" Kevin asked.

"Yes," Frank said. "But the buried treasure hasn't been found."

"*Yet*," Chet added.

Kevin began jumping up and down. "That's it! That's it! The perfect front-page story for the *Pee Wee Press!*"

"What are you talking about, Kevin?" Joe asked.

"I was going to write about the ketchup scandal," Kevin said. "But a story about pirates in Bayport is much better."

"No!" Frank said. "You can't write about this yet!"

"Why not?" Kevin asked.

"Because if all the kids find out, everyone will be looking for the buried treasure," Frank explained.

"Wouldn't you rather write about your friends *finding* the treasure?" Joe asked.

"Sure," Kevin admitted. "But what if you never find it?"

"They'll find it," Chet said. "They're the Clues Brothers, remember?"

Kevin sat down on the steps. He rested his chin in his hands.

"How can I *not* write this story?" he asked. "A reporter has a responsibility to his readers."

"What about your friends?" Frank asked.

Joe folded his arms. "Kevin, if you write this story, we won't go to Pizza Paradise all summer."

"What?" Chet said. He grabbed Joe's arm. "No pizza for a whole summer? Are you nuts?"

Joe glared at Kevin. "And no Italian ices either."

"No Italian ices?" Chet cried. He tugged at his hair. "Arrrgh!"

Kevin paced back and forth. He stopped and looked at his friends.

"Here's the deal," he said. "The deadline for my story is tomorrow."

"So?" Frank asked.

"So I'll give you until three o'clock tomorrow afternoon to find the treasure," Kevin said. "If you don't find it by then, I'm going to write the story."

"You're giving us only one day?" Frank asked.

"To find treasure that's been buried for four hundred years?" Joe asked.

"You *are* the Clues Brothers," Kevin said with a smile.

Frank and Joe looked at each other. Then they nodded slowly.

"Okay," Frank said. "It's a deal."

"Whew!" Chet said. He looked relieved.

"But we're going to have to work super fast," Joe said.

Frank, Joe, and Chet went back to the marina to look for more clues.

"Anybody find anything yet?" Frank called as they walked on the shore.

"Just sand in my sneakers," Joe said.

"And some trash," Chet said. He picked up an old sandy bottle. "I'd better recycle this thing."

Frank looked at the bottle in Chet's hand. Something was stuffed inside.

"Wait, Chet," he said. "There's something in it."

"You're right," Chet said. He shook the bottle upside down. A piece of rolled-up paper fell on the sand.

Joe ran to pick it up. He unrolled it and gasped.

"What is it?" Frank asked.

"It looks like some kind of map," Joe said slowly. "A treasure map!"

5

Dig This!

The boys gathered around the tattered piece of paper.

"A treasure map?" Frank asked. "Are you sure?"

"It says 'Bayport Treasure' on the bottom," Joe said. "And it's got drawings of trees, rocks, and a whole bunch of X's all over it."

"Captain Crook's missing treasure map," Frank cried. "Ye-es!"

Joe was excited, too. "I wonder where it came from," he said.

"I'll bet it's a message from Captain Crook," Chet said. "He's telling us to go for it."

Frank, Joe, and Chet exchanged high fives. Then they spread the map out on the sand.

"How do we know which X marks the treasure?" Chet asked.

"I guess we'll have to check them all out," Frank said with a shrug.

"You mean dig through the whole town of Bayport?" Joe asked.

"You bet," Frank said. "Which means we'll need a good shovel."

"The only shovel we have at my house is a snow shovel," Chet said.

Joe snapped his fingers.

"I know," he said. "Tony Prito's dad is a construction worker. They probably have loads of shovels around the house."

"Good thinking," Chet said. "Maybe he'll lend us a wrecking ball, too."

The Prito house was just a few blocks from the marina. The boys saw eight-year-old Tony dribbling a basketball in the driveway.

"Hi!" Tony called. He pointed to a basketball hoop above the garage. "Want to shoot some hoops?"

"Can't," Joe said. "We're working on a mystery."

"Another mystery?" Tony asked. "What is it this time?"

"First you have to promise not to tell anyone," Frank said.

"What do you think I am?" Tony asked. "A snitch?"

Frank told Tony all about Captain Sid and the buried treasure.

"Wow," Tony said. "Buried treasure in Bayport. Who knew?"

"That's why we need a shovel," Chet said. "A good, sturdy shovel."

Tony waved his hand. "Forget the shovel. I have a better idea."

He put his fingers to his mouth and whistled loudly. His sheepdog, Boof, stuck his head out from behind the house.

"Your dog?" Frank said.

"You bet," Tony said as Boof ran over. "He digs so much in our backyard that he's practically in China by now."

Joe shrugged. "It might work."

"Of course it'll work," Tony said. "I'll even tie a red bandana around his neck. He'll be an official pirate."

"Cool!" Chet said.

After Tony tied a leash and a bandana around Boof, Frank showed him the map.

"I thought we'd check out the X marked on Seabreeze Street," Frank told Tony. "It's right around the corner."

"You hear that, Boof?" Tony said.

Boof kicked up his feet and pulled Tony down the street. Frank, Joe, and Chet followed.

When they were around the corner, Joe studied the map. "The X looks like it's in the middle of the block."

The boys found where X marked the spot. It was in front of a yellow house with a big front yard.

"We can't dig through someone's yard," Frank said. He pointed to a strip of dirt next to the sidewalk. "Let's start there."

Tony gave a big whistle. "Come on, Boof. Do your stuff."

Boof jumped into the dirt. He began digging with his front paws.

"Woof!" he barked.

"Watch it!" Joe shouted as a clump of earth hit him on the forehead.

Frank and Chet coughed as dust and dirt flew all around them.

"Does he have to be so messy?" Chet complained.

"Hey," Tony said. "Do you want to find your treasure or not?"

After a few minutes, Boof stopped. The boys looked down. There was a big hole in the ground but no treasure.

"Bummer," Joe said. "All that digging for nothing."

"Are you sure the map says Seabreeze Street?" Frank asked Joe. "Maybe it was *Breezy* Street."

"Or maybe you were holding the map upside down," Chet told Joe.

"Upside down?" Joe cried. "Do I have a sign on my back that says Stupid?"

The boys were busy arguing when Tony formed a T with his hands.

"You guys," he said. "Has anyone seen my dog?"

Frank, Joe, and Chet looked around. Boof was nowhere in sight.

Suddenly they heard a piercing scream. The boys spun around.

A woman was running out of the yellow house. She had a garden tool in her hand.

"Boof's digging through her flowers!" Joe said.

"Oh, great," Frank groaned.

"Boof!" Tony shouted. He whistled loudly. "Get over here!"

Boof looked up and ran back to Tony. His coat was covered with dirt and flowers.

"That giant furball ruined my gladiolas," the woman shouted from her yard. "My prize-winning gladiolas!"

"I think she's angry," Joe said.

"And she's armed with a weed-whacker," Chet said. "Run for your lives!" Chet began to leap across the hole, but he tripped and fell.

"Are you okay, Chet?" Frank asked.

He looked back at the angry woman. The woman was already busily repairing her garden. She ignored the boys.

"I'm okay," Chet said. "I just tripped over some lump in the hole."

"A lump?" Frank asked.

He kneeled down and brushed away some dirt. Then he felt something hard.

"Hey, you guys," Frank said. "I think I found something."

6

Danger in Store

All right!" Tony cried. "Boof dug up something after all!"

Frank brushed away more dirt. He picked up a round, rusty object. It was about the size of a golf ball but much heavier.

"What's that?" Joe asked.

Frank shrugged. Then he remembered something he had learned in school.

"I think it's a musket ball," he said.

"A what-ball?" Chet asked.

"Hundreds of years ago the guns they used were called muskets," Frank explained.

"They loaded them with musket balls."

"Pirates probably used muskets, too," Joe said excitedly.

"It's a great clue," Frank said.

Chet sighed. "But it's still not the buried treasure chest."

"We're getting there," Frank said. He looked at his watch. "But we'd better call it a day. It's almost time for dinner."

"Let's dig some more tomorrow," Joe said. He looked at Boof. "With a *real* shovel."

"I hear you." Tony sighed. "I hear you."

Boof shook the flowers off his coat. "Woof!" he barked.

That night after dinner, the boys showed their dad the coin, the map, and the musket ball. Fenton Hardy was a detective in Bayport. He often helped the boys with their cases.

"These look impressive," Fenton said. "Why don't you take them to the Bayport Museum to find out if they're real?"

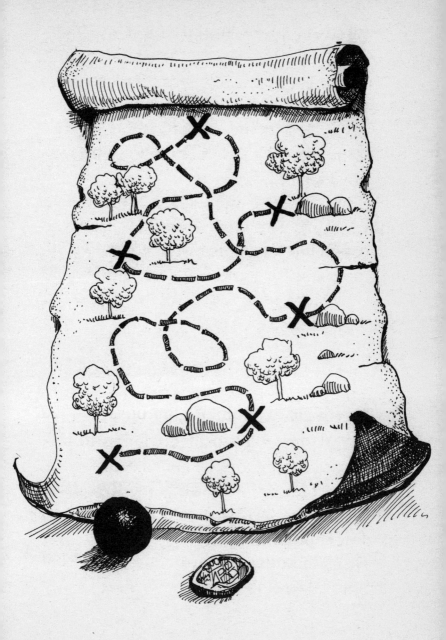

"Oh, we're pretty sure they're real, Dad," Joe said.

"And we don't want word to get out," Frank said. "Until we find the buried treasure ourselves."

Joe smiled. "We'll be so rich, we'll be spitting nickels."

"Hmm," Mrs. Hardy said as she walked into the living room. "Does this mean you boys won't need your allowance anymore?"

Frank and Joe looked at each other.

"Um, Mom," Joe said. "We haven't found the buried treasure *yet*."

Later in the evening it started to rain and thunder. When it was time for the boys to go upstairs to bed, Joe brought his sleeping bag into Frank's room. He wanted to talk about the case before he fell asleep.

"Hey, Frank," Joe said in the dark. "Maybe Captain Crook doesn't want us to find the buried treasure."

"Huh?" Frank asked from his bed. "What are you talking about?"

"Maybe his spirit is mad because Chet splattered ketchup all over his portrait," Joe said.

"Spirit?" Frank laughed. "You don't believe in ghosts, do you?"

"Ghosts? Me?" Joe said. "No way!"

A flash of lightning filled the air. It was followed by a loud boom of thunder.

Joe ducked into his sleeping bag. After a few seconds, he peeked out.

"Not . . . really."

The next morning the rain had stopped. Frank packed all of the clues into a backpack.

After a breakfast of pancakes they met Chet on Marina Lane. He was carrying a small blue plastic shovel.

"That's a sandbox shovel," Joe complained.

"Picky, picky, picky," Chet said. "Now, what's our plan today? I feel lucky."

Frank pulled out the treasure map. He pointed to an X marked under a tree.

"That tree is here by the marina," Frank said. "We can check it out now."

They were about to walk to the tree when Frank stopped. He pointed to Captain Sid's Treasure Cove.

"I have an idea," Frank said. "Let's ask Sid if he'll lend us some pirate stuff. You know, like eyepatches, pirate hats—"

"Why?" Joe interrupted.

"So we can feel like real pirates while we search for the treasure," Frank explained. "It'll be a blast."

They walked over to Captain Sid's shop. There was a sign on the door that read Jumped Ship. Will Return Soon.

"I wonder where he went," Joe said.

"It's too early for lunch," Frank said.

"Speak for yourself," Chet insisted.

The boys pressed their faces against the door to look inside. Suddenly the door swung open. They fell inside in a big heap.

"Ouch!" Chet said from the bottom of the pile. "Get off me!"

Joe rolled off Chet. "I guess Sid doesn't lock his door."

Frank stood up and walked around the dark shop. It smelled like dust and ketchup.

Joe and Chet walked around, too. Without Captain Sid or Horatio, the store seemed pretty eerie.

"Hey," Joe said. He pointed up. "Check out that huge Jolly Roger flag hanging across the ceiling. I didn't notice that the last time."

Frank whistled. "This place is a mess. There's dried-up ketchup everywhere."

"I'll say," Joe said. "It looks like our school lunchroom after a food fight."

"Don't blame me," Chet protested. "Blame Moby Squirt."

Frank saw a stack of pirate hats and a bunch of plastic swords. He began grabbing them.

"Let's pick out some stuff," he said. "We'll show them to Sid when he gets back."

Joe looked through a basket of eye-patches. He felt Chet grab his arm.

"Joe!" Chet whispered.

"What is it?" Joe asked.

"Shhh!" Chet said. He pointed to the portrait of Captain Crook. "The pirate's eyes are moving!"

"Moving?" Joe asked. He stared at the black velvet painting. "They don't look like they're moving to me."

"They are so," Chet insisted. "It's as if he's watching us."

"Be real, you guys," Frank said as he walked over. "His eyes can't be—"

Just then Frank was interrupted by a loud, shrill voice:

"One-Eyed Jack! One-Eyed Jack!"

Frank looked at Joe, then at Chet. "Did anybody say something?"

"Nope," Chet gulped.

"Not me," Joe said.

The voice cried out again, *"One-Eyed Jack! One-Eyed Jack!"*

The boys stared at the portrait.

"I knew it!" Chet cried. "It's the spirit of Captain Crook—calling his ghost ship!"

7

The Whole Loot

I'm outta here!" Frank said.

"Me, too!" Joe said.

"Wait for me!" Chet said.

They turned around and ran. A shadowy figure appeared as they reached the door. Chet crashed into it and screamed.

Frank and Joe stepped back. They saw that it was Captain Sid.

"Looking for something, boys?" Sid asked.

Just then Frank and Joe heard a loud

rustling sound. They looked up and saw Horatio. He was flying out from behind the Jolly Roger.

"One-Eyed Jack! One-Eyed Jack!" he sang. "As a meal or as a snack! Squaaawk!"

"Hey," Frank said as the parrot flew to Sid's shoulder. "That wasn't Captain Crook. It was Horatio."

"And he's singing a jingle for cheese," Chet said. "String cheese."

"Another commercial?" Joe groaned. "Now you tell us."

Frank told Captain Sid why they were in the shop. They showed him the pirate stuff they wanted to borrow.

"We've been looking for Captain Crook's treasure," Joe said. He pointed to Frank's backpack. "We found clues and everything."

Sid's face lit up. "So you're starting to like pirates, eh?"

"We don't really *like* pirates," Frank said. "They used to rob ships, you know."

"I know, I know," Sid said. "It's the adventure you like, right?"

"I guess," Joe admitted.

"Then take this, too," Sid said. He reached for a long black telescope on a shelf. "A pirate never leaves home without his trusty telescope."

"Cool," Joe said, taking the telescope.

"Thanks for lending us all this neat stuff, Captain Sid," Frank said.

"Tacky junk!" Horatio squawked. "Tacky junk! Arrrk!"

Joe rolled his eyes. "Oh, brother."

The boys left the shop. They saw Brian buying a soda at the Salty Dog.

"Did you find the treasure yet?" Brian asked.

"Not yet," Joe said. He looked through the telescope. "But this should help."

Chet slipped on a black pirate hat. "Call us the Bayport buccaneers!"

"Pirates, huh?" Brian asked. Then his face lit up. "I know. Why don't you bring all that stuff on my dad's boat?"

"You mean go for a sail?" Frank asked.

"Sure," Brian said. "What are pirates without a pirate ship?"

"Sounds like fun," Joe said.

Chet shook his head. "I'll pass. I don't want to get sick again."

He handed Brian his hat and plastic sword. Then he turned to the Hardys.

"I'm going back to my house for a pizza muffin," Chet said. "I'll meet you guys here later."

Brian shook his head as Chet walked away. "Whoever heard of a pirate who gets seasick?"

Joe smiled as he thought of a joke.

"What do you call a whale who gets seasick?" he asked. "Moby Sick!"

"Okay, okay." Frank laughed. He raised his sword in the air. "Let's shove off!"

"Aye, aye, Captain Hardy!" Joe said with a little salute.

Mr. Ludlow welcomed Frank and Joe back on the boat. After their life vests were on, he sailed the boat away from the dock.

Frank and Brian pretended to fight with plastic swords.

"You won't plunder my ship, you peg-legged scoundrel!" Brian shouted.

"Give up the loot," Frank shouted back. "Or I'll feed you to the sharks!"

Joe didn't join the battle. He sat at the stern, looking through the telescope. The shore looked close, even though they were far away.

"Land ho," Joe whispered. He moved the telescope back and forth. Suddenly he stopped. He could see something sticking out of the sand. It looked like a big black box.

"Frank! Brian!" Joe called.

Frank and Brian hurried over.

"What do you see?" Frank asked.

Joe looked away from the telescope and blinked. "I think it's a treasure chest!"

"Let me see that thing," Frank said.

He grabbed the telescope and looked through it. There *was* a box sticking out of the sand. And it was right under a tree where X marked the spot.

"Brian," Frank said. "You've got to ask your dad to turn the boat around."

Brian raised his arms. "But—"

"Please, Brian," Frank interrupted.

"Okay, okay." Brian sighed. "But we're never going to sail. Ever."

When Frank, Joe, and Brian were back on the shore, they ran to the box. Frank dropped his backpack on the sand and began to pull at the box.

"Urrrgh," Frank grunted. The box was buried pretty deep, and the ground was muddy from all the rain the night before.

"If it *is* a treasure chest," Joe said, "how come it's sticking out of the ground? Wasn't it supposed to be buried for hundreds of years?"

Frank nodded as he gave the box a final yank. "The rain last night might have washed away some of the sand."

Joe felt his heart pound as Frank dragged the box out of the mud.

"Okay," Frank said. He rested the box on the ground. "Who's going to open it?"

The boys stared at the box. Then they each grabbed the lid.

"It's stuck!" Brian complained.

"What do you expect after hundreds of years?" Joe said. He gave the lid a whack with the telescope.

The lid popped open, and so did their eyes. Inside the chest was a pile of shiny gold coins.

"Hot dog!" Frank cried.

Joe gave a holler. He scooped up a handful of coins in his fist.

"Frank, we're rich!" he shouted. "We're rich!"

"I'm richer!" Brian shouted. He began to dance around the gold. "I'm richer!"

"Wait until we tell Kevin," Joe said.

"We'd better tell him right away," Frank said. He looked at his watch. "It's almost three o'clock."

Just then Frank and Joe saw Chet running toward them.

"Chet!" Frank called. "Look what we found. The whole bounty."

"The mother lode!" Joe shouted.

"Don't get too psyched," Chet said. "I've got bad news."

"Bad news?" Joe asked. "What?"

Chet held up *The Pirates of Bayport*. "Iola finally let me read this book. The Bayport they wrote about is somewhere in the Bahamas."

"The Bahamas?" Frank said. "You mean that—"

Chet nodded. "There were no pirates here," he said.

"No pirates?" Joe asked slowly.

"If that's true," Frank said, "then what about the clues we found?"

"And the treasure we just found," Joe asked. He pointed to some red streaks inside the lid. "See? That's probably blood from a pirate battle."

"Blood?" Chet asked. He ran his finger along the stain and sniffed it. "That's not blood. It's ketchup."

"Ketchup?" Joe cried.

Brian shrugged. "Maybe Captain Crook liked cheeseburgers."

Frank examined the stain. "It looks kind of fresh. Not hundreds of years old."

"I've got some more news for you guys," Chet said. He unwrapped a coin and popped it in his mouth. "These coins aren't gold. They're chocolate!"

8

Finders Keepers

This isn't the time for corny jokes, Chet," Frank said.

"Would I joke about chocolate?" Chet asked. He handed Frank a coin. "Try one. They're milk chocolate crunch."

"Chocolate coins?" Brian wailed. He unwrapped a coin. "This isn't treasure. It's pirate junk food."

"Wait a minute, you guys," Joe said. "If this treasure isn't real, then what about all the other stuff we found? Like the silver coin, the musket ball, and the treasure map?"

"Someone's been planting all this stuff," Brian said.

Frank stared at the ketchup stain. Then he jumped up.

"Captain Sid's store was splattered with ketchup from Moby Squirt."

"Yeah, so?" Joe asked.

"Ketchup . . . treasure . . . Captain Sid's Treasure Cove!" Frank said.

There was a loud squawk in the tree above them, then singing.

"Captain Sid's, Captain Sid's! Come to shop and bring the kids!"

The boys looked up as Horatio flew out of the tree. But he didn't land on any of their shoulders. He flew straight to Captain Sid.

"Ahoy, boys," Sid said. He peeked out from behind another tree. "I see you found the loot."

"You call this loot?" Frank asked as Sid walked over.

"It is if you like chocolate." Captain Sid chuckled.

"Ah-ha!" Joe said. He pointed a finger

at Sid. "So you planted the fake treasure."

"And the fake clues," Chet added.

"They *were* fake, weren't they?" Brian asked.

"As fake as a pirate's peg leg," Sid admitted. "I drew the treasure map and buried the clues when business was slow. Which is just about always these days."

Joe was disappointed. He thought he liked Captain Sid. How could Sid be so sneaky?

"You did all that to trick us?" Joe asked. "How come?"

"I just wanted you boys to have a little fun," Sid said. He gave a wink. "You did have fun, didn't you?"

The boys looked at each other. Then they each broke out laughing.

"I guess we did," Joe said.

"And we learned a lot about pirates, too," Chet said.

"There's just one problem," Frank said. "How are we going to tell Kevin that there weren't any pirates in Bayport?"

"I don't know," Brian said. "I just hope he didn't rip up that ketchup story."

Frank reached into his backpack. He pulled out the coin, the musket ball, and the treasure map. He was about to hand them back to Sid when he stopped.

"Wait a minute," Frank said. He showed Sid the silver coin. "You were still in the shop when we found this yesterday. How could you have planted it then?"

"Yeah," Joe said. "We found it right after we ran out."

"Coin?" Sid asked. "I didn't plant any silver coin yesterday. Let me see that."

Sid took the coin from Frank. He looked at it and whistled.

"It looks like you boys found a real pirate's piece of eight," he said.

"Piece of eight! Piece of eight!" Horatio screeched. "Arrrk!"

"You mean . . . treasure?" Joe gasped.

"How do we know for sure?" Chet asked.

Frank took the coin from Sid. Then he

68

smiled. "There's only one way to find out," he said.

The boys went straight to the Bayport Museum, where they got their answer—the coin *was* an authentic pirate's piece of eight.

"I guess we found treasure after all," Frank said with a smile.

Joe smiled, too. "And we didn't even need a shovel!"

Two weeks later Frank, Joe, Chet, and Kevin celebrated at Pizza Paradise. The pizza parlor was decorated like a pirate ship with Jolly Roger flags and fishnet curtains.

"Just think," Joe said. "There really were pirates in Bayport."

As the boys waited for their pizza, Kevin held up a copy of the *Pee Wee Press*.

"So, guys," he said. "How do you like my front-page story?"

Joe read the headline out loud: "Clues Brothers Find Pirate Loot."

"I like it just fine," Frank said.

Brian took the paper from Kevin and stared at the headline. "It sure beats the ketchup story," he said.

"And the best part is," Frank said, "the Bayport Museum is hanging a plaque with our names on it. Right next to the pirate coin."

"That's not the best part," Chet said.

"What is?" Joe asked.

Chet reached into his pocket. He pulled out a fistful of chocolate coins. "Sid let us keep all the chocolate!" he said.

Mrs. Saris came over holding a pizza pie. She was dressed in a pirate costume.

"Yo, ho, ho, boys!" she said. She placed the pizza on the table. "Here's your grub."

The boys looked down at the steaming pie. It smelled like fish and was covered with gobs of stringy green stuff.

"Mom?" Kevin asked slowly. "What kind of pie is this?"

Mrs. Saris smiled. "It's Pizza Paradise's

pirate special—topped with anchovies and lots and lots of seaweed."

"Anchovies? Seaweed?" Chet gulped. He looked at his friends. "Hey, guys? Is it possible to be seasick when you're still on land?"

Frank and Joe laughed. From now on their summer would be smooth sailing—all the way!

**Do your younger brothers and sisters
want to read books like yours?**

Let them know there are books just for them!

THE
N A N C Y   D R E W
N O T E B O O K S ®

Look for a brand-new story every other month

Available from Minstrel® Books
Published by Pocket Books

1356-09

The Hardy Boys are:

THE CLUES BROTHERS™

#1 The Gross Ghost Mystery
#2 The Karate Clue
#3 First Day, Worst Day
#4 Jump Shot Detectives
#5 Dinosaur Disaster
#6 Who Took the Book?
#7 The Abracadabra Case
#8 The Doggone Detectives
#9 The Pumped-Up Pizza Problem
#10 The Walking Snowman
#11 The Monster in the Lake
#12 King for a Day
#13 Pirates Ahoy!

By Franklin W. Dixon

Look for a brand-new story every other month

A MINSTREL® BOOK

Published by Pocket Books

1398-08

Sabrina
The Teenage Witch™

Salem's Tails™

What's it like to be a powerful warlock,
sentenced to one hundred years in a
cat's body for trying to take over the world?

Ask Salem.

**Read all about Salem's magical
adventures in this new series based on the
hit ABC-TV show!**

#1 CAT TV
#2 Teacher's Pet
#3 You're History
#4 The King of Cats
#5 Dog day Afternoon
Salem Goes to Rome

Now available!
Look for a new title every other month

A MINSTREL® BOOK
Published by Pocket Books

2007-03

TAKE A RIDE
WITH THE KIDS ON BUS FIVE!

Natalie Adams and James Penny have just started
third grade. They like their teacher, and they like
Maple Street School. The only trouble is, they have
to ride bad old Bus Five to get there!

#1 THE BAD NEWS BULLY
Can Natalie and James stop the bully on Bus Five?

#2 WILD MAN AT THE WHEEL
When Mr. Balter calls in sick,
the kids get some strange new drivers.

#3 FINDERS KEEPERS
The kids on Bus Five keep losing things.
Is there a thief on board?

#4 I SURVIVED ON BUS FIVE
Bad luck turns into big fun
when Bus Five breaks down in a rainstorm.

BY MARCIA LEONARD
ILLUSTRATED BY JULIE DURRELL

A MINSTREL® BOOK
Published by Pocket Books

1237-04